Ashley Wolff

Only the Cat Saw

Puffin Books

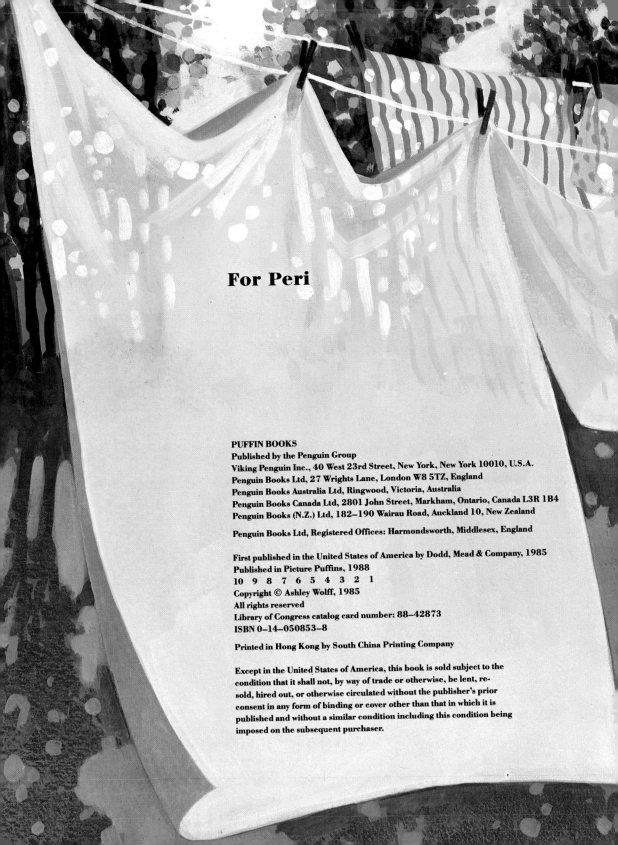

For Peri

PUFFIN BOOKS
Published by the Penguin Group
Viking Penguin Inc., 40 West 23rd Street, New York, New York 10010, U.S.A.
Penguin Books Ltd, 27 Wrights Lane, London W8 5TZ, England
Penguin Books Australia Ltd, Ringwood, Victoria, Australia
Penguin Books Canada Ltd, 2801 John Street, Markham, Ontario, Canada L3R 1B4
Penguin Books (N.Z.) Ltd, 182–190 Wairau Road, Auckland 10, New Zealand

Penguin Books Ltd, Registered Offices: Harmondsworth, Middlesex, England

First published in the United States of America by Dodd, Mead & Company, 1985
Published in Picture Puffins, 1988
10 9 8 7 6 5 4 3 2 1
Copyright © Ashley Wolff, 1985
All rights reserved
Library of Congress catalog card number: 88–42873
ISBN 0–14–050853–8

Printed in Hong Kong by South China Printing Company

It was suppertime
and night was coming soon.
Mother was busy with Sam.
Amy was helping Father.
So only the cat saw…

At bath time

Father was singing to Sam.

Mother was tickling Amy.

So only the cat saw...

At bedtime

Mother and Father were reading.

Sam was finally asleep, and

Amy was supposed to be.

So only the cat saw…

At midnight
Amy was dreaming.
Mother, Father, and Sam
were sleeping.
So only the cat saw...

At two o'clock in the morning

Amy got up very quietly.

No one else did.

So only the cat saw...

A few hours later
Sam woke Mother.
Amy and Father slept on.
So only the cat saw…

It was breakfast time,
and day had begun.
Mother was washing her face.
Sam was watching Father.
And the cat was sound asleep.
So only Amy saw...

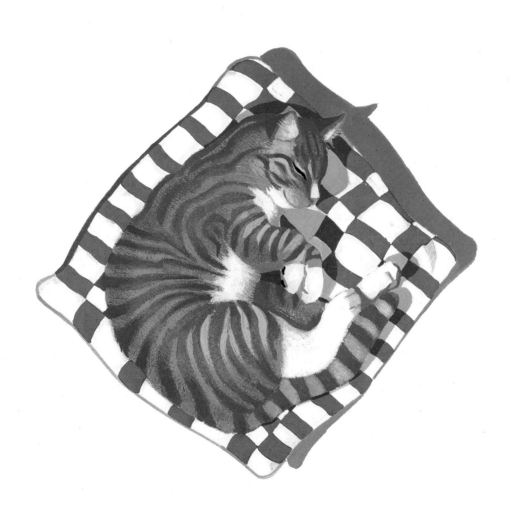